a FIRST MYSTERY book

MY DOG and the BIRTHDAY MYSTERY

by David A. Adler
illustrated by Dick Gackenbach

Holiday House / New York

Text copyright © 1987 by David A. Adler
Illustrations copyright © 1987 by Dick Gackenbach
All rights reserved
Printed in the United States of America
First Edition

Library of Congress Cataloging-in-Publication Data

Adler, David A.
My dog and the birthday mystery.

(A First mystery book)
SUMMARY: With the help of her dog, Jenny spends her
birthday investigating a bicycle theft and wondering
why no one seems to remember it is a special day for
her.
    [1. Birthdays—Fiction. 2. Dogs—Fiction.
3. Mystery and detective stories] I. Gackenbach, Dick,
ill. II. Title. III. Series: First mystery.
PZ7.A2615Mu 1987   [E]   86-14269
ISBN 0-8234-0632-6

My name is Jenny.
This is my dog.
My dog has four legs,
two in the front
and two in the back.
She has white curly hair
with lots of black spots.
And she is really very smart.
My dog solves mysteries.
I couldn't think of a good name
for my dog
so I just call her My Dog.

One day I was sitting in my backyard.
It was my birthday.
My mother gave me
a make-it-yourself model
of an airplane.
My father gave me glue.
I was putting the airplane together
when My Dog wagged her tail
right into the tube of glue.
"That's not a very smart dog," someone said.
I looked up and saw my friend Ken.

I thought he came to wish me
a happy birthday
and to give me a gift.
I was wrong.
"I need you to help me
solve a mystery," Ken said.
"My bicycle was on my porch.
It was locked and now it's gone."

My Dog barked.

I knew what she wanted.

"My Dog thinks

you must have loaned the bicycle to someone."

Ken shook his head and said, "No."

"But if your bicycle was locked,

how could anyone take it?" I asked.

Ken said, "That's what makes this a mystery."

My Dog barked.

I knew what she wanted.

"My Dog says

you should take us to your porch."

Ken said, "Oh no,

don't bring your dog.

She'll only get in the way."

"No she won't," I said.

"My Dog will solve your mystery."

When we got up to follow Ken,
one of the airplane wings
stuck to the glue on My Dog's tail.
I pulled the wing off.
My Dog whined a little.
It hurt.

I took along my pad and pencil.
As we walked,
Ken described his bicycle.
Green with two wheels,
I wrote on my pad.
One wheel in front and one in back.
A little bell, a seat and a basket.
On Maple Street,
my friend Jane walked past us.
She was carrying a large bag.
My Dog barked.
I smiled at Jane
and waited for her to wish me
a happy birthday.
She didn't.
She just walked by us.
She seemed to be in a hurry.
My Dog began to follow Jane.
"Come here," I called.
My Dog barked.

She looked up at Jane.

"Go on. Go to Jenny," Jane said.

My Dog looked at Jane and barked.

"Go on," Jane said. "Go on."

"Come here, My Dog," I called.

My Dog ran back to me.

"That's not a very smart dog," Ken said.

"She thought Jane was you."

Ken showed me his porch.
He was right.
His bicycle was gone.
But the lock and chain were still there,
and they were closed.
"This is a *real* mystery," I told Ken.
"How could someone take your bicycle
without opening the lock?"
I looked for clues.

My Dog looked too.
Ken's porch is really big.
It runs across the front of the house
and along one side of the house, too.
There were no clues
on the front part of the porch,
just some popcorn.
My Dog ate it.

Then I saw my friend Lisa walk past.

"Hi, Lisa," I said.

Lisa knew it was my birthday.

I had told her.

"Do you know what today is?" I asked.

"Sure," she said. "It's Tuesday."

She seemed to be in a hurry.

Lisa went down the walk
of the house next to Ken's.

That's Ellen's house.

Ellen is my *really* good friend.

My Dog began to follow Lisa.

"Come here," I called.

My Dog looked up at Lisa.

"Go on. I'm not Jenny.

Go on," Lisa said.

My dog ran to me.

"Your dog is dumb," Ken said.

"She follows anyone."

"She is not dumb," I said.
"My Dog will solve your mystery."

"Come with me," I told My Dog.
"We have to find more clues.
  We have to find Ken's bicycle."
I looked on the porch.
My Dog looked too.
She found a trail of popcorn.
It went from Ken's porch,
  down the steps and along the front walk.
As My Dog followed the trail,
  she ate the popcorn.
There weren't any clues
  on Ken's front porch.
But on the side porch,
  I found baby powder.
"I wonder who spilled that," Ken said.
  I told him,
"I don't care who spilled it.
  Look what went through it."
There were bicycle tire marks
  in the powder.

"Some powder must have stuck
   to the wheels," I said.
"Look, there's a trail of powder
   up to the edge of the porch.
   I followed the trail.
"Look," I said again.
"Whoever took your bicycle
   carried it off the porch right here."

I followed the trail,
and Ken followed me.
The trail led right to Ellen's house.
I didn't think my friend Ellen
would steal a bicycle,
but I had to follow the clues.
I knocked on Ellen's door.
"Come in," Ellen said.
I opened the door.
"I'm in the den," Ellen said.
I walked through the hall
to Ellen's den.
It was dark.
Someone had pulled down the shades.
"Ellen, Ellen," I called.
Someone turned on the lights.

Then people were all around me.
They were jumping and yelling "Surprise"
and "Happy Birthday."
All my friends were there.

"Is this party for me?" I asked Ellen.

"I just came here looking for Ken's bicycle."

Ellen told me,

"Ken's bicycle is in his garage.

He put it there.

He said it was missing,

and he spilled the powder

so you would come here.

This is a surprise party for you."

I looked around.

Balloons were tied

to the lights.

On the couch were boxes

wrapped in gift paper.

On the table were bowls

of jelly beans, cookies,

gumdrops and popcorn.

In the middle of the table

was a large birthday cake.

Ellen told me that
Barry brought the jelly beans,
Lisa baked the cookies,
Jane brought the gumdrops,
and she baked and iced the birthday cake.
And Ken said, "I made the popcorn."
"That's why there was popcorn
on your porch," I said.
"There was a trail of popcorn
from Ken's house to mine," Ellen said.
"And your dog followed it.
She came in
when I opened the door for Barry."
"Where is My Dog?" I asked Ellen.
"In the kitchen," Ellen said.
"I put her there because
I didn't want her to eat
all our candy and cake."
I went into Ellen's kitchen.

My Dog was standing on a chair
and drinking water from Ellen's sink.
I brought My Dog into the den.

"My Dog solved your mystery,"
I told Ken.
Then I told all my friends,
"My Dog knew that you made me
a surprise birthday party.
That's why she came here."

"Oh, your dog didn't know that,"
  Barry said.
"She just followed popcorn."

"Look at your dog now," Ken said.
My friends all looked at My Dog and laughed.
My Dog was sitting on the chair
and eating the paper and ribbons
off my gifts.

Ellen put her arm
around my shoulder and said,
"We all like you,
and we like your dog.
But she isn't very smart.
She'll eat anything."
I smiled and said,
"So will I."
I ate some cake,
popcorn, jelly beans,
cookies and gumdrops.

Then I sat next to My Dog,
and while she chewed on a big red bow,
I pretended to nibble on
a small piece of gift paper.